The Inkwell

The Inkwell

TIM BROWN

RESOURCE *Publications* · Eugene, Oregon

THE INKWELL

Resource Publications
An Imprint of Wipf and Stock Publishers
199 W. 8th Ave., Suite 3
Eugene, OR 97401

www.wipfandstock.com

PAPERBACK ISBN: 978-1-6667-3039-5
HARDCOVER ISBN: 978-1-6667-2183-6
EBOOK ISBN: 978-1-6667-2184-3

JUNE 25, 2021

This book is a work of fiction. Any references to historical events, real people, or real locales are used fictitiously. All characters appearing in this work are the product of the author's imagination, and any resemblance to actual persons, living or dead, is entirely coincidental.

Library of Congress Control Number: 2020905736
First Edition: August/2020
10 9 8 7 6 5 4 3 2 1

DEDICATION

This book is dedicated to our patriots, my fishing buddies, and everyone else who believes in miracles.

The Escape

CHAPTER ONE

Seven generations of Reed descendants had been guardians of the inkwell. The small glass bottle was a coveted family keepsake from the Revolutionary War. The empty, glass vessel sat on the mantel, housed beneath a domed-glass cover that nested into a polished mahogany base. He removed the glass dome, carefully grasped the inkwell, and placed it in the pocket of his khaki fishing pants. The inkwell was the lynchpin in Major Abram Reed's escape from British captivity. Major Reed was Jerry's fourth great grandfather and Jerry felt privileged to have been the inkwell's keeper for almost forty-five years.

Jerry Reed had a decision to make. He was five-years retired, and it was time to decide which member of the next generation would be the inkwell's keeper. A day earlier, he and his wife, Mary, had canceled an appointment with their attorney. They had planned to finalize their will. Jerry simply was not ready because he couldn't decide which of his three children would receive the inkwell. To find clarity, as he put it, he called three of his retired friends and made plans to go fly fishing. Mary wasn't angry because of the changed plans, but she secretly wondered if Major Reed knew how much unnecessary worry he had caused by keeping the inkwell rather than throwing it in the river, the river that had carried him to safety. She didn't notice the inkwell was not in its designated place on the mantel until Jerry was gone.

Before retiring, Jerry owned and operated Reed's Clothing, a clothing store for men. Dr. Chuck Radcliff was a dentist with an agreeable, take-charge personality. He was also a playful agnostic, often at Sammy's expense. Sammy McCartney was a cabinet maker and devout Christian. Jerry, Chuck, and Sammy met while attending a fly-tying class almost twenty years earlier. Don, a retired high school principal and die-hard environmentalist, joined them several years later, as a church friend of Jerry's who always wanted to try fly fishing. Their differences kept things interesting. Their love of fly fishing was the high ground that kept things friendly.

Jerry was the glue that held the group together. He was their deliberate, soft-spoken, organizer, and self-appointed fly-fishing fashion consultant. He was sure the right shirt and the right hat would help him catch fish. He said little and fished well.

Fly fishing is a simple and solitary sport. A fly rod, a hand-tied fly, a gin-clear stream, and an ever-present measure of hope are all that's required. Of course, getting to the water and relaxing after a day of fishing requires company. It's been said that if you dislike community, beware of solitude. Conversely, if you dislike solitude, beware of community. That's why Jerry liked fly fishing with his three longtime friends. It provided both solitude and community.

By its nature, fly fishing requires space. Even a simple, thirty-foot cast requires a significant back cast and room to float the fly. Standing in a stream, with a fly rod in hand, demands that even good friends must be separated. There is space to be alone, though, when you catch a fish, you must expect quick questions from fifty feet away, like, "What are you using?" And, "What color is it?" You may have to raise your voice over the noise of the fast-moving water to be heard, but you answer. Then you return to your coveted bubble of trout-stream solitude. You are alone until you choose not to be.

Jerry's go-bag was always packed, and his fishing gear was neatly organized. It took him no time to load his Grand Cherokee. He picked up Chuck and Don around 6:30 a.m., and they began the two-hour drive to their favorite stream, a remote tributary of the Niangua River in southern Missouri. Sammy could not join them on such short notice because he planned to spend the day staining his deck. It was an unusually quick-turn trip for the three retired friends, which was the first topic of conversation.

"Damn, Jerry, you came out of the blue on this one. We were lucky to find a place to stay. What got into you?" Chuck asked. "What's the matter, Jerry. Did you tick off Mary again?"

"Oh, I needed some by-myself-think-time and being with you two is damned near like being alone," Jerry answered, not yet ready to share his inkwell dilemma.

"Come on, man. You're the planner among us. Expecting spontaneity from you is like expecting to catch a trout tagged with a winning lottery ticket. You would never suggest a fishing trip on such short notice unless you had a reason," Don added.

"Okay, okay, okay. We've been finalizing our will, and that sort of thing poses questions that are hard to think about, let alone answer. I just thought a day on the stream would help me focus. I'm glad you guys were free for my emergency fishing trip."

"Emergency fishing trip? That's an oxymoron," Chuck said.

"I'll bet we could work that into a great bumper sticker," Don added.

"Have you guy's written a will?" Jerry asked, unwilling to let lighthearted conversation sidetrack him.

"Yep. We did that about five years ago," Don answered. "Seemed pretty cut and dried to me. Of course, we've added three grandkids since then, and we need to include their names on the list. But that shouldn't take long. In fact, we can probably do it over the phone. Are you worried about who is going to get your favorite fly rod?"

"Nope. My inkwell."

"You're what?"

"There's a family story that I have probably never told you. You know how people's eyes glaze over when you start talking about your dead relatives. But I have an inkwell with a remarkable story behind it. It has been in the family since the Revolutionary War, and I cannot decide who should get it next."

"An inkwell with a remarkable story? Let's have it, and it better be good. I sacrificed big for you today," Chuck kidded. "I planned to fill the car up with gas and change my dog's flea and tick collar."

Even though the group was one man short, the familiar presence of two friends was welcome and comforting to Jerry. Quiet Jerry was going to be more talkative than usual, as he told the story of Major Reed and the inkwell.

"My fourth, great grandfather was Major Abram Reed. Well, he wasn't always a Major. When the inkwell event happened, he was a twenty-five-year-old Lieutenant. He was taken prisoner by the British in September of 1777, and because he was an educated man with excellent penmanship, they made him a captive scribe in their headquarters office, which was little more than the living room of an occupied farmhouse on the Mohawk River in north-central

New York. The farmhouse sat very near the river. Each day he was escorted from the dirt-floored barn that he shared with fourteen other prisoners. He and his fellow patriots had been held captive in the heavily guarded barn for two weeks before a British officer learned of Grandpa Reed's writing abilities. Once they did, they escorted him each day to the headquarters office to transcribe day reports, letters, and other official military documents."

"See what a good education will do for you," Don interrupted.

"That and plenty of courage took him a long way," Jerry answered. "You see, as their transcriber, he developed an arms-length, but respectful, relationship with the commanding officer, whose handwriting was close to illegible. Grandpa Reed had to ask the Colonel to decipher his handwriting often. They had many polite, civil conversations, which didn't sit well with the corporal who guarded Grandpa Reed as he worked. That didn't matter much to Grandpa. In fact, the guard's foul attitude about the friendly relationship between his prisoner and his commanding officer was what led to Grandpa Reed's escape.

"He worked late one night. He was to transcribe a letter for the Colonel, but his ink was too thick. He asked the guard to get him some water to dilute the gummy sludge that coated the bottom of his inkwell. The guard answered, 'Get your own goddamned water.' That late in the day, the water pitcher and basin were empty. The nearby river was his only option. Grandpa lifted the inkwell from the ornate, silver inkstand, stood up, and headed for the door. He had no coat, no hat; only the inkwell. As soon as the door closed behind him, escape seemed remarkably possible. He walked briskly to the river's edge, bent down, added water to the inkwell, and glanced behind him. Seeing no one, he turned around to face the house, placed the inkwell in his pants pocket, and walked backward slowly into the chilled darkness of the stream. One push into the steady current of deeper water, and he was on his way to freedom. He swam, waded, and floated for nearly six hours. At daybreak, he stopped to rest on the river's bank, and, eventually, he found his way behind American lines and was reunited with his company."

"And you have the inkwell?" asked Chuck. "I mean the same inkwell. I'm surprised he just didn't throw it away."

"He thought about it. In fact, as he repeated the story in later years, he admitted that the little bottle caused him concern. He said that he was amazed at how many fast-paced thoughts can race through your mind during a time of extreme danger. Rather than pocket the bottle, he considered leaving it on the riverbank so that the British wouldn't pursue him to recover it. Then he laughed at himself. If they chased, they would chase him, not the bottle.

"He did say that he had one regret. Once in the water, the gummy residue in the bottom of the little bottle became ink again. It leaked and left a six-inch black stain on the right leg of his trousers. He was disappointed at first. He loved those pants, even though he had worn them every day for over a month. Over time, the stained trousers took a place of honor just behind the inkwell. He never wore them again. He stored them, neatly folded, in the corner of his war chest, which held other war-time memorabilia, including the empty inkwell. He asked his family to bury him wearing those stained trousers when the time came. That's what they did. His coffin covered his lower half, so nobody noticed."

"Give it to the Smithsonian and be done with the burden," Chuck said. "You are assigning too much importance to the damned thing.

"No, I can't do that. I must respect the wishes of the generations of people who have had it before me. It's amazing that I have it. It has been many places over the years. It's lived in the corner of a musty trunk; it's been displayed with a small Confederate flag protruding from it. Once, it housed a bullet slug. Grandpa Archi Reed had a duel with a political rival in 1833. He was hit, though the bullet glanced off a metal clasp on his suspenders, hit a rib and traveled around his rib cage, and came to rest under the skin just beneath his left arm. He survived. His rival did not. Archie was the inkwell's keeper at the time, and he kept the recovered slug in the little bottle. The slug was lost along the way, but thanks to the bottle and Archi Reed's willingness to document the incident, we know about still another stop in the inkwell's generational travels."

"What was the duel all about?" Don asked. "It is hard to believe that people actually settled things in such a way. I'll bet you had to be awful damned mad to do it."

"I never got totally to the bottom of that. Archie was a newspaper editor in Nashville. Seems he wrote something negative about a man who was running for the U.S. Senate, and the fight was on."

"Dueling was around long before Grandpa Archie. At one time, people thought that it was a good way to settle disputes because God himself decides who survives," interrupted Chuck. "Just another example of the hogwash that can come from believing in an imaginary god."

"Chuck, you are just full of information, aren't you?" Don kidded.

"Yes, sometimes, I am."

"Hey, Chuck, did you find a church yet?" Jerry interrupted.

"Stop," Chuck snapped.

"You'll figure it out. You'll figure it out," Jerry said with grinning reassurance.

"So, which way are you leaning, Jerry? Who is going to be the next inkwell keeper? Will it be Julia, Robert, or young Josh?" Don asked. Jerry's three children were unevenly spaced. Julia was the oldest at twenty-six. She was a nurse. Robert was a twenty-three-year-old college student. Then came Josh. He was sixteen and a pleasant surprise. Jerry was fifty-two when he was born.

"That's the question that lies before us," Jerry said. "It will be answered with your help before we head home tomorrow."

"Wait just a minute, my friend. This is your decision, not ours. Don't lay your moldy, ancestral dilemma on us," Chuck demanded.

"And just what are fishing buddies for?" Jerry smiled as he said it.

The Inkwell Knows

CHAPTER TWO

They put thoughts about Grandpa Reed and the inkwell on the back burner for the remainder of the ride. They talked about sports, politics, lawn-mower maintenance, and the high cost of pharmaceuticals. It was a pleasant trip, and Jerry was curiously relieved after sharing his dilemma with his friends. They arrived near the river about 8:30 a.m. but, before fishing, they stopped for breakfast at Margie's, a fisherman's diner about three miles from the river's edge.

As they walked toward Margie's front door, Chuck noticed Jerry's new hat. "Whoooeee, look at that fancy, new hat. That's nice. You look like a professional fisherman," Chuck kidded. "Combined with that baby-blue fishing shirt that you got last year, that hat makes you look like a dude straight from the pages of an Orvis fly-fishing catalog. Better hurry and get it dirty, so you don't look like a rookie."

For a fly fisher, there is no such thing as too much equipment. These fishermen had everything they would ever need to successfully catch a trout. Still, when they saw some new gadget, piece of clothing, or fly-fishing accessory that

15

would make their buddies even slightly envious, they bought it. Despite his caring demeanor, Jerry was the catalyst for this friendly competition. One year, it was new khaki fishing pants. The next year, it was the vented blue shirt. This year, Jerry had a brand-new hat, and he was glad Chuck noticed. It was a boonie hat, with a four-inch, floppy brim and a leather drawcord, which dangled beneath his chin.

"Mary told me it was time for me to take the sun seriously. This should protect my ears and neck just fine."

"Don't let Margie see it. She'll want to take your picture. Damn, you look good," Chuck said with a playful wink. Soon enough, the new hat was forgotten, and they concentrated on breakfast.

Chuck looked up from his biscuits and gravy with an idea. "Why don't you make a list of personal attributes that you think the next inkwell keeper should have. Then ask yourself which of your kids fits best."

"Been there, done that," Jerry replied. In fact, Mehitable Reed, Major Reed's daughter-in-law, made such a list back in 1802, after it was apparent that Grandpa's story might become a family thing. She wasn't the keeper, but her list of guidelines evolved into a journal of stories and instructions that accompanies the bottle. Each keeper adds a few pages as it's passed along. That's how we learned about Uncle Archie's duel and the bullet slug. The journal is something else that worries me. My contribution to the journal will be downright boring. Six people have been keeper before me. Of course, not all of them added memorable stories to the book, but I always hoped I'd have a compelling story to tell about my time as keeper. Sorry, no jailbreaks or pistol duels here. I mean, what do I have to tell? I graduated from college. Got a job in a clothing store. Finally bought the clothing store. I sold clothes. I saw neckties go from wide to skinny to wide again at least three times. And I fly fished. Now, isn't that some legacy?"

"I'm sure you've got some fly-fishing stories that will keep them interested," Don suggested. "Reminds me of my Great Aunt Leona's diary, which we read after she passed. It was chock full of everyday activity. Boring, really. Then we turned the page and found a silly, little poem that made us all laugh. There wasn't another thing entered on that day. That stupid poem was like a long, slow wink from Aunt Leona. We all knew her a little better because of it. Jerry, your contribution to the journal will be excellent. Just let them know who you are."

"Spoken like the teacher that you are, Donald," Chuck interrupted. "Let's get back to old Mehitable. What did she say about the important attributes of the inkwell keeper? What is the most important thing that an inkwell keeper should be?"

"Most important; Mehitable said that the person should be literate," Jerry explained. "Then, she said that the keepers should love history and draw strength from learning about the lives of their ancestors. Well, my kids are all literate. Which of them is best prepared to become their generation's family historian is the question. All of them love the story of Grandfather Reed, I think. In fact, Josh made a presentation to his sixth-grade class about him. I even let him take the inkwell to school for his show-and-tell."

"That may be your answer," Don suggested.

"Yeah, but it was an assigned class project. I don't know how much stock to put in it."

"Then why don't you sit them down and let them vote. Let them decide," Chuck said.

"It's the keeper's decision. That's one of Mehitable's rules. It's a good rule. It fosters a sense of responsibility for one of your last decisions as a keeper.

"Part of the problem is how to evaluate the kids. Julia's the oldest. She's responsible, caring, and bright. But totally preoccupied with her love life. I'll bet she is married within the year. Robert is a perennial college student. He is a great guy, with lots of friends. Too many, perhaps. He's too committed to having a good time right now. Josh is just sixteen. He's a good student and has shown an interest. Still, comparing them is difficult because they all are at such different points in their lives. The bottom line is simple. It must be the one who will handle the responsibility best over the long haul."

Jerry thought about showing his friends the inkwell then but decided to wait. "I wish Sammy were with us. Sometimes things just fall out of his mouth that surprise the hell out of you," Jerry concluded, and then changed the subject. "Let's go fishing," he said.

Thirty minutes later, they were in the water up to their thighs. Jerry took the rougher water just beneath a small waterfall. The water only dropped about three feet over the rocky ridge, but it caused enough churn to make keeping an eye on a dry fly challenging but interesting. Then the water pooled into what they called the Blue Hole. Chuck took the front of the pool, and Don took the far end, where the water turned shallow and choppy because of a pea-gravel sand bar. No one said a thing. No jocular bets on the first fish were offered. No bravado challenges based on earlier successes or failures were uttered. These men were friends who instinctively separated themselves from one another to fish and to seem to be alone.

Jerry gave up on the dry fly after ten unhurried casts and tied on a nymph to fish deep. He watched Chuck land a respectable rainbow, and he immediately returned to the camaraderie of the community.

"What were you using?" Jerry shouted.

"Thread jig," Chuck answered.

"What color?"

"White."

The conversation was unnecessary because a white thread jig was Chuck's go-to fly, and both Jerry and Don knew what he would be using that early in the day. If he had answered otherwise, they would have known he was lying. Later in the day, especially if fishing was difficult, Chuck's willingness to be totally honest might have been tested. Oh, he wouldn't have lied exactly. He would simply have mumbled something unintelligible and kept on fishing. On a trout stream, the real measure of friendship is not the promise of honesty. It is the unspoken understanding that the fish-catching friend will be asked questions. They'll be asked solely to give the successful fly fisher the satisfaction of knowing he is envied.

It was Don's turn. He had shortened the drop from the strike indicator to the tiny nymph and let his line drift to the shallow end of the pool and into the riffles. A large rainbow took the fly with authority. It didn't nibble, it attacked. The fight was on. Don's high-pitched giggle let the world know of his success. He was the newest to the sport and was still amazed he could catch a fish on a such a tiny hook. He compared his zebra midge to a nail clipping from his little toe. It was a small hook that could become dislodged if the fly fisher didn't pay attention to detail. Maintaining patient pressure on the fish was critical. If the fish wanted to run, he would let it run. Then retrieve. Let it run and retrieve it again. The idea was to tire the fish so, when it was time to land it, the exhausted fish would float effortlessly into the net without incident. A green fish will invariably make a mighty, last-ditch leap and dive, which can break the line because the shock-absorbing bend of the rod is already spent. That leaves the once-euphoric fisherman muttering an off-color oath over an empty net.

Despite his preservationist ways, Don had a quirky habit. He always played a fish much longer than necessary, and his fishing buddies teased him mercilessly about his deliberate slowness. When he finally netted a fish, it was virtually comatose. Jerry thought that he was deliberately slow because he didn't want the fun of the catch to be over. Whatever the reason, today was no different. Don played the fish beyond tiredness.

"Better land it now, Don," Chuck teased. "It's going to be dark in a couple of hours." Don landed the fish. Chuck smiled and showed his appreciation with a congratulatory nod. Jerry smiled too. He had seen it all before. The day seemed to be shaping up just like he'd planned.

They were all surprised by the voice from the high bank behind them. "Whoopee! That is a nice fish. Good thing you landed it. It's only two hours until suppertime," Sammy said.

"Well, look who's here!" Jerry shouted back. "Welcome, Sammy." The band of fishermen was complete.

"I decided I could paint anytime. So, I took a chance and came on down. I thought I'd find you here. Is Don the only one who is doing any good?"

"Chuck has one. And I'm picky. I'm waiting for a lunker," Jerry said.

"He can't concentrate on fishing because he's too worried about his Grandpa's inkwell," added Chuck. "Don't ask him about it now. It'll take longer for him to tell you about it than it takes Don to land a fish. Get your rod. Maybe you'll bring Jerry some luck."

Sammy was back inside of fifteen minutes with his boots on and his rod ready. He waded in just beyond Don's protruding sand bar. There, the water pooled again in front of a car-sized rock and then wrapped around the boulder into a wide sweep of unobstructed water. The four men fished without speaking for nearly an hour, except for the obligatory what-are-you-using exchange. They all caught fish, though the action slowed some for Don. He changed flies four times and caught nothing more. Finally, another fish took his tiny fly. Jerry needed a break, so he waded ashore and motioned to Chuck to do the same. They stood on a low rise directly behind Don, anticipating the predictable, twenty-minute fight between Don and his fish. Sammy saw what they were up to and joined them.

"Great fish, Don. He's staying deep; it must be a big one. Don't horse him in, now. Just be patient and let him run if he wants to," instructed Jerry.

"Don't let him up in those riffles," Sammy added. "If you do, you'll have to fight the current and the fish."

"If he runs straight at you, take up line as fast as you can. You may want to strip it with your left hand, rather than the reel. Too much slack and he's gone," Chuck admonished.

The fish didn't run at him. It torpedoed away from him for about forty feet, breaking the water's surface with a mighty leap that ended with a flat-slap landing that left them all breathless. It was a huge fish. Don's tormentors didn't say another word until the fish was in his net. It took well over twenty minutes, and with good reason. It was a five-pounder, at least. It lay across the net's frame for a heart-stopping moment before folding and falling to the bottom of the net.

"Nice job," Chuck shouted. "You've become a master."

"Remarkable," said Sammy. "Simply, remarkable."

Jerry said nothing until he removed his digital camera from his waterproof vest pocket and asked Don to turn and smile. Don did, holding the net high with the huge, spent fish lying motionless in the bottom of the net like a pot-bellied man snoozing in a drooping hammock.

"After that, I think it's time to take a break," Jerry sighed. I know you just got here, Sammy, but Don and his lunker just plain tired me out."

Don smiled wide. "I agree," he said, as he gently lowered the tired fish into the stream with his hands. He cupped his left hand loosely under the fish's belly, carefully clutching the tail section with his right hand so that he could push the fish forward and then pull it backward slowly. That gentle movement allowed cool water to pass through its bright-red gills. He pushed and pulled the fish several times. The great fish welcomed the moving water and slowly revived. As it did, Don released it. The fish swam away slowly, uncertain of its freedom. Then, with one thrust of its tail, returned to the depths of the Blue Hole.

As they walked back to their cars, Chuck said, "Gosh, Don, I thought you might want to keep that one and mount it. Of course, I realize that might violate your oneness-with-nature standards. By the way, are you related to Henry David Thoreau?"

"Oh, yes. He's my third-great-uncle. In fact, I have a bird's nest and an acorn that he passed down to me," Don quipped. "But, that fish? No, I couldn't keep him. He was too much fun. Besides, Uncle Henry would have pestered me all night if I had."

Chuck ribbed Don relentlessly about his environmental concerns when Don first joined the group. The teasing occurred far less frequently in recent years. But when it resurfaced, Don could always hold his own. He might have been newest to the sport of fly fishing, but he came with an inherent respect for mother nature. He worked in the public-school system for over thirty years, yet he insisted that nature is our best instructor. He said it teaches the importance of gentle care. And, because it has its own clock that cannot be slowed or hurried, it teaches us patience.

Jerry, Chuck, and Sammy were not heathen, but their imagined need to gather food prevailed until Don joined them. Eventually, their need to tease was replaced with respect for the new perspective which Don gave them. Every good fisherman understands the need for patience.

Once at the car, Chuck revisited Major Reed. "So, Jerry, is your head clear enough to solve your inkwell problem?" he asked.

"Not yet, but we have another day of fishing to get there, don't we?"

"Okay. It's time to tell me what's going on," interrupted Sammy. What's the deal with this inkwell?"

Jerry retold Major Reed's escape story, ink-stained pants, and all. He also explained his dilemma about passing the inkwell torch.

"Chuck wanted to be scientific about it by making a list of attributes to measure the kids against. Don thought democracy was in order. He suggested that I let the kids vote on it. You know, let them decide. Both ideas have merit, but I want to think a little longer. After all, I set the record as the inkwell's keeper. No one has held the responsibility longer than I have."

"Really. I guess life spans are longer these days," Don said.

"That, and the fact that it was given to me when I was very young. My dad died when I was just twenty-two years old."

"Has it ever gone to a woman?" Sammy asked.

"Yes, just one of them. In fact, she was the person I beat out for the longest tenure as the keeper. She had it for thirty-eight years. Her name was Silvia Miller. While she had it, she thought it was charmed. She and her husband almost perished in a house fire in 1850. They were awakened by a barking dog and managed to escape the flames. They didn't have a dog. There was another strange thing that occurred when they returned to the burned-out ruins. Almost nothing much was salvageable, except the inkwell. It sat on the mantel, and, like the fireplace and chimney, the inkwell remained standing. It was blackened by smoke, but totally unharmed. The journal was too. It was in a metal trunk in the basement, along with her wedding dress and some tintype images of her wedding day. They were also unharmed. She put the barking dog and the invincible inkwell together and decided that Major Reed's relic had protective powers. Major Reed was saved. Grandpa Archie was saved, and so were she and her husband."

"You believe her?" Chuck asked.

"Well, I don't think it's surprising that three keepers had traumatic events in their lives that seemed connected to the inkwell but to suggest that they avoided death or ruin because of the inkwell's magical powers is a bit of a stretch," Jerry replied. "Eventually, she went off the deep end with her inkwell spiritualism."

"How so?" Don asked.

"She began doing readings for people, using the inkwell as sort of a crystal ball. At first, she kept them private. People came to her new home and sat across the kitchen table from her. She placed the inkwell in the center of the table. Then, with her thumbs touching, she would partially encircle the inkwell with her hands. The guest would do the same from the other side of the table, touching Silvia's fingertips with their own. The guests were instructed to say nothing, but to think of a question that could be answered with a 'yes' or 'no' response. Silvia would sit quietly for several minutes, eyes closed, fingertips lightly touching those of the guest, and eventually answer 'yes' or 'no.' Some left elated. Some left crying. Silvia charged fifty cents for a reading."

"Did she write all this down in the journal?" Chuck asked.

"No, her brother, Amos Reed, did, mostly to explain her eventual reputation as a nut-case."

"Nut-case?" questioned Sammy.

"Yes. Things came unglued for her when she went public. She rented a spot at the Harvest Festival to sell pickles. She didn't sell pickles. She did readings under a hand-lettered banner that read, 'The Inkwell Knows.' Most people thought she was crazy, but she did attract quite a crowd. There she sat, right alongside the other ladies with their homemade jelly, rhubarb pie, bread and butter pickles, and creamed horseradish, giving readings. Her husband was so embarrassed about it that he asked his friend, the sheriff, to gently shut her down. The sheriff took her home, after a stern warning not to violate Harvest Festival directives again. Later, her husband and her brother tried to convince her to give up the job as keeper. They failed. She continued to do private readings, but the die was cast. Most folks continued to think she was touched-in-the-head. Her brother became the keeper after she passed."

Sammy responded slowly, knowing that what he was about to say would cause Chuck to wince. "It just never works to try and force your way into the other side," he said. "Silvia isn't the first or the last to try. People feel a little divine nudge or observe some hard-to-explain events and they get all worked up and try to force the issue. It's just not how things work. If God wants you to know something, he'll find a way to tell you. He might even use an inkwell to do it, but it's his call, not ours. Yep, God can become a presence in your life in any way he chooses."

"So, you think that the life-saving events that Silvia attributed to the inkwell are evidence of divine intervention, rather than some hocus-pocus power of the inkwell?" asked Don.

"Just a thought. Reminds me of my own grandma's story about thin spots," Sammy added.

"Thin spots?" asked Jerry.

"How does all this help Jerry solve his problem?" interrupted Chuck. He sensed Sammy was about to spout some of his usual, inane spiritual wisdom.

"Sorry, Chuck. I know that kind of talk makes you uncomfortable. Maybe later, when you're asleep, I'll tell the others about thin spots. And you're right, involving God in this question may not be necessary. It could be that Jerry doesn't have a problem at all. Jerry already knows who he's going to choose. He is just playing with the decision like Don plays a fish. He simply doesn't want to choose his successor because he is having so much fun being the keeper."

"Say that again, Sammy," Jerry asked. He tried not to show his annoyance. "You think I've become so neurotically obsessed with the inkwell that I don't want to give it up? Is that what you are saying?"

"Jerry, I don't know anything for sure. But doesn't it make sense? You've been the keeper for over 45 years, and you're the one who has all the journal stories memorized. You're the one who people turn to so they can recharge their ancestral memory. Am I right? There's nothing at all wrong with taking it seriously. But, darn it, Jerry, you're not going to die tomorrow. All you're doing is writing a will. You're not resigning your position as keeper. Even though it might feel like it, you're not."

Sensing the tension, Don interrupted, "Hey Sammy, did you notice Jerry's new hat?"

"Of course, I did. But I'll be darned if I was going to say anything about it," Sammy responded with a smile.

Everyone was silent. Community stings sometimes. They return to the stream.

The Nickname

CHAPTER THREE

The Reed's home was a four-bedroom English Tudor, which sat on a tall-treed cul-de-sac in one of the town's older subdivisions. They had lived in the house for over thirty years, longer than any of their neighbors. They were good neighbors and made friends easily. One family, the Dawson's, left the neighborhood for a newer home years earlier but remained good friends with the Reeds. Arlene and Roger Dawson kept in touch.

Mary sat the table with Arlene in their small, but nicely appointed kitchen. They were more than old neighbors. They were very close friends who loved to play verbal hopscotch and prank one another.

"More iced tea," asked Mary.

"No, thank you. I want to be home before Roger gets there. That way, I'll be busy in the kitchen when he starts complaining about his lousy golf game. I don't know why he doesn't take up a hobby that doesn't frustrate him so. Like, maybe, fishing. Is Jerry still a fisherman?"

"He is. In fact, that's where he is today. He and two of his buddies went south to their favorite trout stream. Said he needed some time to think, and he says he can do that best on a trout stream."

"Time to think? What's bothering him?

"Oh, it's that darned inkwell," Mary said. "You do remember our family's fabled inkwell story, don't you?"

"Of course, and I remember the day I heard it." Arlene rolled her eyes as she said it.

"That sounds like a story all its own. What happened?"

"I changed my mind. I will have a little more tea."

Mary got up, retrieved the pitcher of tea from the tidy counter, refilled Arlene's glass, and sat down. "So, what was so memorable about your introduction to the inkwell story?"

Arlene sipped tea and gathered her thoughts. "I think we'd lived next door for about a month. You asked us over for dinner, and all went well until the inkwell caught my eye. I spotted it sitting there on the mantle under its protective glass dome. I was underwhelmed. It looked like such an unimportant little thing to be given such a high perch, but I figured if someone displayed such a modest item in such a prominent way, they would want to talk about it. So, I asked Jerry, 'What's that all about?' He looked at me with a curious smile for the longest time. I instantly knew I should have been a little less cynical with my question. It was like he was trying to understand if I was a smart ass or if I really wanted to know about his little bottle-under-glass. I guess he decided that it was a story I needed to hear. Jerry asked me to sit. Then he talked for fifteen minutes about Grandpa somebody who escaped from the British with an inkwell. It was a remarkable story. But, honestly, I remember his intensity in the telling more than the story itself."

Mary nodded. "He chooses his audiences carefully. He really doesn't talk about it much, unless someone asks. That was your mistake. You asked. He has two versions. One's short. One's long. You got the long one. That means he likes you. But I am glad you told me. Now I understand his nickname for you."

"Nickname? Jerry has a nickname for me. What is it?"

"I'm not sure I should tell you."

"Oh, come on. We've been friends for a long time. You can tell me anything."

"Well, okay. Don't be angry. When Jerry sees you coming, he says, 'Here comes the smartass.'"

"Really!"

"Gotcha!" Mary laughed and winked.

"You bum! I should have seen that coming. But, what's his concern about the inkwell?"

"He's worried about who should be the next keeper of the inkwell. He can't decide which of the kids is the best person for the job. He's so perplexed about it that he canceled our meeting to finalize our will. We'd had the appointment for a month, and then he cancels because of his indecision about that one question. Then, he ran off with his fishing buddies to focus. That was his word. He said he needed to focus."

"I don't understand how a trout stream will help him focus, but what do I know? But, really, isn't he making a mountain out of a molehill? I mean, couldn't you just leave that line blank, finish the remainder of the will and complete it with a phone call after he makes up his mind?"

"That's what the attorney said. But Jerry's determined to complete this task, once and for all. I just wish he didn't see it as a task. It should be a celebration, and it probably will be when all is said and done. But when Jerry becomes obsessed with an issue, I know enough not to get in his way. I'm sure he'll work it out. He always does."

"Gee, that's a side of Jerry I've never seen."

"I suspect that the issue isn't which kid's the best choice. The issue is Jerry's resistance to the very notion of not being the inkwell's keeper. He just doesn't want to give it up. I reminded him that he is only preparing a will, and he's not giving up anything. He didn't hear me. Like I said, he'll discover that truth in his own way. It takes time, but he always does."

They heard the front door open.

"Josh. Is that you?" Mary raised her voice to be heard.

"Hi, Mom," Josh answered. "Is Dad home?"

"No. He's fishing. Come in here and see Arlene."

Josh placed his backpack on the marble-topped table in the hallway and entered the kitchen. He poured a glass of iced tea and joined his mother and Arlene at the kitchen table. Almost a man at sixteen, he was tall, trim, and self-assured. He was a three-sport athlete and a co-captain of the junior debate team. People often commented on his maturity and the ease with which he spoke with adults. He'd known Arlene all his life. She was like family. "Hi, Mrs. Dawson. You and Mr. Dawson doing okay?"

"We're both doing fine. And I was just leaving to go start his dinner. Gosh, Josh, you look good. It's great to see you." Arlene got up and headed through the living room to the front door. Mary followed.

Arlene took a quick glance at the mantel on her way, stopped, turned, and walked straight across the Persian rug to the fireplace. Hoping to even the score after Mary's nickname jibe, she hatched a scheme to offer playful reverence to the all-important inkwell enshrined on the mantel. She took one look at the empty dome and had to change her plan. "So, where's the inkwell now?" she asked.

"Isn't it there?" Mary walked quickly toward the fireplace. She stood before the empty dome totally bewildered. "I don't know. Jerry must have moved it for some reason, or maybe he took it with him. He's been acting weird about the thing lately, but why would he take it fishing? Unless he didn't take it," Mary paused. "You took it, didn't you. What did you do with it?"

Arlene laughed. "Mary, I've been in the kitchen drinking tea with you the entire time. How could I have taken it? I'd love to say 'Gotcha.' But I am not that quick, and I am certainly not guilty. Besides, you brought up the darned thing, not me. Think about it."

"Of course, you're right. But it is a mystery. Oh, I'm sure there is a good reason for its absence, and I'm not going to worry about it," Mary said, returning her attention to her friend. "It was great to catch up. Thank you for coming over."

"I hope you find your inkwell," Arlene said, as she went out the door. As she walked toward her car, she turned and said, "Call me when you do. I'm interested."

Mary nodded, waved, closed the door and spoke to Josh, who had picked up his backpack and was heading toward the open staircase. "You didn't move the inkwell, did you?"

He turned and said, "No, I didn't, but it's what I wanted to talk to Dad about. When is he coming home?"

"Tomorrow night. The phone coverage is sketchy where he usually fishes but, if he calls, I'll be sure you talk with him. Is it anything I can help you with? Is there something you want me to tell him, just in case you aren't here when he calls?"

"No. It's no big deal. It'll wait until he gets home. I just wondered if he'd care if I retyped the Inkwell Journal. As it is, some of it's typed, some of it's hand-written, and it's all becoming very fragile. I just thought it would be nice to have it all in one document that wouldn't need to be handled with such care."

"Sounds like a good idea, but you're right. You'd better talk to your dad first." Mary said. She glanced at the empty dome on the mantel. Despite her assurance to Arlene, the void did worry her.

CHAPTER FOUR

The guys had seldom seen Jerry with his feathers ruffled. Sammy's remark about Jerry's real reasons for his inkwell-keeper procrastination didn't land softly. Jerry remained distant and introspective.

"What are you using?" Don asked Chuck after Chuck landed two fish within ten minutes.

"Fish are rising. I'm using a dry. A Crackleback with an orange body. Try it. If something doesn't take it while it's on top, strip it slowly toward you as it reaches the end of its arch. If you need one, I have extras," Chuck answered. Then, realizing that he may have sounded a little too chummy, he added, "But you'll have to come get it. I'm not going to bring it to you." Nobody felt like lying that afternoon, though being cheeky was still okay.

"No need. I have one, I think."

They all caught fish that afternoon. The solitude was welcome, broken only by fish-speak, and even that didn't happen very often. It was near dark when they stopped.

"Are we eating at Margie's tonight, or did you guys bring something to grill," asked Sammy.

"Margie's it is. We barely had time enough to pack our rods, let alone buy food. Jerry came out of the blue on this one," Don said. Then, realizing he had landed close to the wound, he added. "I'm glad he did, though. This sure beats staining a deck, doesn't it?"

"Margie's special is her tenderloin sandwich. It isn't healthy, but it sure is good. Better than most things we'd grill, and we don't have to do dishes," Chuck added.

Margie saw them coming and greeted them with her usual happy chatter. "Well, if it isn't my favorite fishermen sneaking in here just before closing time. Damn, someone here smells like fish. That you, Jerry?"

Jerry's gloominess evaporated instantly when confronted with Margie's contagious cheerfulness. "It's not me today, Margie. Today was Don's day. He caught what must have been a five or six-pounder. He's ready for his Lunker Sundae." If one of Margie's fly fishers caught a fish that weighed three pounds or more, it was considered a lunker. That earned the lucky angler an embarrassingly large Lunker Sundae. Jerry showed Margie the picture of Don and his netted great fish, and it was all the proof she needed. He had earned a Lunker Sundae. It was a five-scoop, ice-cream mountain covered with hot fudge and crushed peanuts. It had a little plastic trout stuck on the top. They took pictures with Margie's camera and with Jerry's. The group shot of the four fishermen surrounding the sundae was the most fun. Don held a dripping spoonful of ice cream to his mouth as the others looked on with hungry envy. It had been a great day of fishing. Don's Lunker-Sundae picture would soon be thumbtacked to Margie's bulletin board alongside images of other lucky winners.

"Where are you staying tonight? I brought an air mattress and a sleeping bag. Can I use your floor?" Sammy asked.

"No need. We have a cabin at Ralph's. We have four beds, so we're set. Of course, we'll have to tell Ralph that we are adding a man. If we don't, he'll sick that damned dog on us and kill us all," Jerry explained. Ralph owned and operated a ten-cabin lodge about a mile down the river road from Margie's. It was not their preferred place to stay, but the last-minute decision to fish required a small sacrifice. Ralph and his wife, Beulah, and a disagreeable, mongrel dog, named Rattler, ran the place. Jerry was not surprised that they had rooms available. Ralph and Beulah both had the vacant personalities of seasoned prison guards. They were a good match. Add the slobbering, crossbred dog, and you had a trio of foulness that did little to encourage repeat customers. The four fishermen stayed at Ralph's Cabins several times, usually when they were unable to find room elsewhere. Even so, it became an oddly appreciated part of the fishing-trip experience. Ralph, Beulah, and Rattler were the brunt of dozens of jokes and observations.

They stayed in unit number four, a spartan, no-frills, one-room cabin with a cold tile floor and dirty, knotty-pine paneling. "Ralph is such a grump. Do you think he might just need a good laxative?" Don asked, after they all crawled into bed.

"I think he is as regular as clockwork," Chuck responded. "Beulah is the one I worry about. She sits back there at her little desk, with a lit cigarette dangling from her lip, pretending to do something. What do you think she's doing? I'll bet she's carefully picking the spot for the shallow grave they'll need for next the disappearing guest."

"How'd you like to have a duel with Ralph. I think he'd cheat. Hey, Sammy, did you know that Chuck is an expert on duels?" Don asked.

"Duels?"

"You know, where guys draw their guns and fight to the death, like Jerry's Grandpa Archie."

"It isn't always guns," submitted Chuck. "Sometimes its swords. In fact, Abraham Lincoln was challenged to a duel after he called someone a smelly, foolish liar. Abe chose swords to take advantage of his long arms. Then he apologized, and the duel was canceled."

"Like I said, Chuck. You are so full of information."

"Now, children. Calm down. It's time to get some sleep so we can enjoy the Magic Kingdom tomorrow," Jerry scolded. Then he reduced his voice to a loud whisper. "Besides, we must remain quiet so we can hear Beulah as she draws near with a tranquilizer gun and Ralph's chainsaw. Now, turn out the light."

Chuck wasn't ready to sleep. "You know, I think if Beulah was going to do something dreadful, only God could stop her."

"Did you say God?" Sammy pipped up. "You gave God credit for doing something?"

"Sure, if Jerry can imagine tranquilizer guns and chainsaws, I can imagine a job for your imaginary god."

"He will get you for that," Sammy said.

"Hope he does it after breakfast. Margie's pancakes are to die for."

"You know, Chuck, the Bible's Paul was kind of a hard case too. Look what happened to him," Sammy kidded.

"I don't have scales on my eyes, fellas. I can see perfectly well."

Sammy was surprised that Chuck was aware of the story of Paul's conversion. He brought it up as conversational bait. Maybe, just maybe, Chuck would ask him what the hell he was talking about, and he would have reason to tell the story. Now, knowing that Chuck knew all about it, he said, "Listen to us long enough, Chuck, and our favorite fishing spot might become your trout stream to Damascus."

Jerry sensed that his friend's bed-time teasing was developing a harder edge than usual. He changed the subject. "Don't worry, Sammy. Chuck will figure it out. He'll figure it out. Hey, Don. What are you using tomorrow, a midge, or a dry fly?"

"I haven't decided yet. There is too much noise in here to think."

Once again, fly fishing high ground saved the day. Sammy was closest to the light. He turned it out and listened for Ralph's chainsaw for about five minutes before drifting off.

The next morning, they fished upstream from the Blue Hole at the place they called the Cliff Hole. It was a long stretch of smooth water in front of a forty-foot-high rock wall. The water closest to the wall was deep and interrupted by small grassy islands. Over time, large rocks had fallen from the wall and gathered moss, silt, and other fertile river debris. Above the water, the rough edges of those fallen boulders were smoothed by aquatic vegetation. The rocks became the foundation of alluring, green bulges in the smooth-flowing stream. Some even had sapling trees growing from them. Beneath the water, they formed the perfect resting place for hungry trout, which hid in the protected water and then shot into the open stream to ambush breakfast when it floated by.

With the morning sun against the wall and their backs, it was a glorious place to begin the day. It was Don's favorite spot. He loved to contemplate its formation, almost as much as he loved to fish it. He cast his forget-me-knot nymph within inches of one of the grassy mounds. He watched the orange strike indicator move slowly around the submerged rock and then sink quickly.

"Fish on!" he shouted. There would be no time to coach him through his slothful retrieve that morning. Chuck and Sammy had a fish on, too. When their splashing subsided, Jerry also met success. Each man was totally reassured of his superior fishing skills before 9:30 a.m.

"What a morning of fishing!" Chuck yelled. "Let's go have breakfast."

Their rods carefully stowed, and wet boots piled high in the bed of Sammy's extended-cab pick-up, they were off to Margie's. She never worked in the morning, so they didn't have to deal with her effervescent personality. They took a booth by the window. Jerry purposely didn't sit next to the window so that he could stand, when necessary. It was his turn to revisit the inkwell discussion, and they all knew it. They would discuss the morning's success, talk about their hottest flies, and complain about the quality of the coffee until he did. He didn't keep them waiting.

"Well, Sammy. I must praise you for your insight and thank you for your honesty," Jerry said through a sincere smile. "You were right. At least, mostly right. While it is important to pass the keeper responsibility to the right person, the reason I was wrestling with the decision had more to do with me than any of my kids. I am, as you suggested, having a hard time giving it up. And it goes a step deeper than that. I don't like thinking about my own mortality. Preparing a will sets you thinking. I'm sorry I got off on such a personal tangent. Next time we fish, one of you guys can be the one on the couch."

"It's a great story, Jerry. I'm glad you shared it with us," Don said. "I've never had much interest in my own roots. I think I'll do some digging."

"You may be surprised by what you find. I was lucky enough to have much of mine handed to me, accompanied by an inkwell. And speaking of inkwells, look at this."

Jerry stood up. He placed his hand into the right-hand pocket of his khaki fishing pants. He carefully removed a small, squeaky-clean, glass bottle and set it in the middle of the table. Jerry watched the expressionless faces of his friends as they stared at the inkwell. The daylight glimmered through the window and highlighted the imperfect, wavy glass beneath its fluted lip. Still, it was just an empty bottle. It was not awe-inspiring. In fact, it could have been placed alongside the salt and pepper shakers and never been noticed.

"Well, how-do-you-do," Chuck said. "That's it. That's the coveted inkwell?"

"That's it," Jerry said, sitting down. "And nobody knows the trouble it's seen."

"You do, and now we know some of it."

"That's what I meant. Just to look at it, without knowing where it's been, it's nothing special at all. When you imagine the hands that have held it, it takes on its own personality, doesn't it?" Jerry responded. His enthusiasm for the inkwell was unabated, even in the face of his new understanding of his self-centered procrastination.

"So, have you decided which one of your kids will be the next keeper of the inkwell?" Sammy asked.

"Yes. It'll be Josh. At least, that's who it goes to now. If I change my mind next year, I'll choose someone else. Sammy was right about that, too. I am not going to die tomorrow. I have time to change my mind. I've been making this problem bigger than it deserves to be."

"A good night's sleep has done wonders for you, Jerry," Chuck laughed.

Breakfast came. Jerry grabbed the inkwell and returned it to his pocket. They decided they would return to the Cliff Hole after breakfast. They'd had too much fun there, not to. The late-morning fishing was slower. They fished for about twenty minutes when Jerry left the water and walked the bank toward Don. "Hey, Don, I'm going to get out of these waders and fish the Blue Hole. It's easier to fish from the bank there. My stomach's getting a little grumbly and getting out of waders in a hurry is never fun, if you get my drift. You guys stay put and fish. I'll be there when you're ready to go. I think two o'clock is a good time to shoot for."

"Hey, I've got some Pepto Bismol in my bag. It's the side pocket. Help yourself if you need it."

"Na, I'll be okay. I just want to take it easy for a while."

"Okay," Don said. "I'll tell the others."

Jerry walked back to the Blue Hole, went up the hill to the cars, and changed out of his waders. His canvass walking shoes felt good. He walked down the narrow path to the gradually sloping, sandy beach and to the water's edge. He stripped out a length of fly line and made a perfect dry-fly cast toward the bank on the deep side of the stream. The fly landed gently and began its slow drift with no tell-tale drag. It was an artificial fish feast there for the taking. His stomach was still uncomfortable, but he felt better until he noticed pressure growing in his chest and pain that seemed to radiate down his left arm. Then the chest pressure became a solid, full-fisted punch. He dropped his rod and stumbled forward three steps into knee-deep water. He turned and faced the shore to return to the dry land. He could not step forward. He staggered backward three more awkward, splashing steps and dropped into the chilled rush of the deeper water. He felt its steady, unrelenting current engulf him, and he was on his way to freedom.

Don was first to see Jerry's boonie hat floating downstream. "Hey, is that Jerry's hat? He must have dropped it." The hat floated in the deep water, close to the green-domed rocks. It was impossible to retrieve from where they were fishing, and they watched it bump the green mounds like a descending ball in a pinball machine and float away quickly. They would have to walk downstream and find a shallower catch point. Then they saw a fly box afloat on the stream. The buoyant box was closer to them than the hat had been. Sammy waded out, netted it, and popped it open. It was Jerry's.

"This isn't right. Let's go!" yelled Sammy.

"Don, you take the high path. It's faster." Chuck shouted. "We'll stay close to the shore. If you find something, blow this," he said, as he tossed Don an emergency whistle. "Blow one long, if everything is okay. Give us three shorts if you need help. Do it as many times as you need to. Just be sure we hear you."

The high path was straighter and faster. It was the quickest way to the Blue Hole, but it did not allow an uninterrupted view of the winding stream. Splitting up allowed them to cover both the stream and the Blue Hole, in the least amount of time. Sammy had his own whistle, so they were all equipped to signal, if necessary.

Chuck and Sammy walked quickly with their eyes glued to the river. Don jogged the high path at a steady pace. He reached the Blue Hole, panting, in five short minutes. He saw nothing of Jerry. He climbed the hill and checked the cars. Jerry's wet waders and wading boots were in the bed of Sammy's pickup. He ran back to the stream and started up the winding shoreline path to meet the others. That's when he heard their whistle. It shrilled three times in sequence, and then three times again. He swallowed hard and hurried. They were close. As he rounded a lazy curve in the stream and ducked under a low-hanging branch, he saw them, not thirty yards away. They were on the river's bank frantically removing their waders. He ran toward them and saw the pitiful reason for their haste. A man's right elbow intermittently poked through the water's surface, as the current thrust the man's submerged body against a partially sunken tree in which it was entangled. A baby-blue shirt-sleeve covered the bobbing arm.

Sammy saw him coming, cupped his hands, and yelled, "Call 911. Take my truck. Keys are under the floor-mat. Drive toward Margie's and watch your phone for a signal. Should be able to call about halfway there."

"Is he gone?" Don yelled back.

"Don't know. Now go!"

Chuck and Sammy waded in stocking-footed, knowing that they would have to swim the last ten yards to reach Jerry. Sammy got there first, grabbed Jerry's arm at the elbow, and tugged. The arm straightened and bounced back to its original position. Jerry didn't budge. Chuck swam behind Jerry's submerged body, treaded water, and reached beneath the surface to grab anything he could touch. He found Jerry's net, then fingered his way along the net cord, which was attached to Jerry's vest. Grasping the vest, he took a deep breath and allowed himself to sink beneath the surface so that his feet touched bottom. It was slick but solid. It gave him leverage. He yanked hard. That's all it took. Jerry's still-buoyant body surfaced and began a swift curl with the current around the tree limb. Sammy stopped him, though the current wanted to possess Jerry's lifeless body as much as Sammy did. Chuck surfaced and swam to assist. They turned Jerry face-up to keep his nose and mouth above the surface. Each took a side; Sammy on the left, and Chuck on the right. With one hand grasping Jerry's blue-shirted torso and the other plunging through the water in a determined, single-handed breaststroke, they swam to shallow water and dragged him to the river's edge. Jerry's upper body was out of the water as Sammy began chest compressions. His legs remained submerged.

"Wait a minute, Sammy. I want to see if he has a pulse." Chuck panted. He placed his fingers on Jerry's neck. He shook his head and said, "Go ahead, we have to try. But, let's get him out of the water first." They both took an arm and pulled Jerry toward the flat, dry ground. That's when they saw it.

"What the hell is that! Chuck snapped, as he peered down at Jerry's khaki fishing pants. There was a six-inch black stain on the right leg of the trousers that seemed to emanate from a lump in Jerry's pocket. Sammy instinctively plunged his hand into Jerry's pocket and removed the inkwell. He examined it. It was clean. He put it in his vest pocket and zipped the pocket tight. He said nothing and resumed chest compressions. When Don and the rescue team arrived, they were sitting exhausted with Jerry's body on the flat stretch of shoreline. Jerry's head was in Sammy's lap, his net and fishing vest tossed aside. The paramedic confirmed what they already knew. Jerry was gone.

As the rescue team placed Jerry's body on the stretcher and prepared to cover him, Chuck spoke. "Please, wait a second, guys. Don, say goodbye to Jerry." Then, with a gentle nudge, he encouraged Don to step forward for a final look at Jerry. It was a curious suggestion, but he did as he was told. He noticed the black stain on the pant leg immediately.

"What's that?" Don blurted, pointing at the blemished right pant leg.

"Looks like some kind of a stain," the paramedic responded. "Looks like ink or something."

Don turned and faced his fishing buddies. The three men stared at each other in unspoken wonderment.

Chuck broke the silence. "Okay if we take his trousers?" he asked before he considered how odd the request sounded.

The paramedic hesitated, looked quizzically at the three devastated fishermen, and, although he realized their sincerity, he could not honor their request. "I'm sorry, I can't do that," he said.

"Well, you must promise us that those pants will make their way home with him," Sammy added.

"I can promise that. They will accompany him home."

"Are you guys going to notify his wife, or is that up to us?" Don asked.

"We'll do that," the paramedic responded. "We have his wallet. If you guys have his home number, it would be a big help." They picked up Jerry's vest and followed the stretcher-bearers back to the Blue Hole, traded his number for Jerry's car keys, and went back to the stream to gather their scattered gear, including Jerry's rod.

Don drove Jerry's car home, and Chuck rode with Sammy. It was a silent ride. About an hour into the trip, Chuck couldn't help himself. "It must have been tar or something. It could not have been ink. I hate mystical stuff like this. I hate it. There has to be some explanation for that stain."

Sammy answered, "There is, but you won't believe it." After that, the silence returned.

A Thin Spot

CHAPTER FIVE

The three men met at a convenience store on the outskirts of town to gather their thoughts before taking Jerry's car home and talking with Mary. Josh was standing in the doorway when the two cars pulled into their driveway. He turned and called his mother.

It was a difficult meeting. After hugs and condolences, they sat down in the living room. Mary quietly asked, "Can you tell me what happened?"

"Sure, but do you mind telling us what the coroner reported when he called?"

"Not much. He said that it first looked like Jerry drowned, but he doesn't think so. He suspects a heart attack. They will know more tomorrow."

"That would make sense. Jerry was feeling ill. His stomach was upset. He left the three of us so he could fish in a more comfortable spot, a spot where he wouldn't need to wear his waders. Maybe a half-hour later, we saw his hat floating by us," explained Don. They told her all they could, without mentioning the ink-stained pants or Jerry's angst about choosing a new keeper of the inkwell. They decided not to tell all until Jerry's fishing pants were available to help confirm their story. "Mary, we'd like to know more about the coroner's report. I'll call you tomorrow. Then we would like to talk again. There may be some blanks we can fill in after we've had time to think. Right now, we'd like to go home and let it all sink in."

Mary knew that they were holding something back, but she realized that their day had been nearly as rugged as hers. She agreed. The following morning, she received his call.

"Hi, Mary. This is Don. Is this a good time to talk for a moment?"

"Yes, of course."

"Did you talk with the coroner?"

"Yes. He said it was a heart attack, a massive one."

"I'm not surprised," Don said. "Did they deliver Jerry's things to you?"

"No, but they said I could pick them up."

"How would it be if we picked them up and brought them over? That would give us a chance to talk further. We have Grandpa Reed's inkwell and some information to share with you."

That would be fine. I'll have to call the coroner's office to clear it, but that would be fine. What's going on, Don? What is it you aren't telling me?"

"I'm sorry, Mary. Please, bear with us on this. It's not bad news. It's just an unusual circumstance that accompanied Jerry's death. It is best explained in person. Is there a good time that we can meet with you again? Will your children be with you this afternoon?

"Why don't you come by about three o'clock. Josh will be here, but he will respect our need for privacy if we ask him to."

"That's great, Mary. We'll see you then. Believe me, this will interest you, but it should not worry you. We'll see you at three."

They picked up the package of Jerry's personal effects. They didn't open it until they were sitting in Mary's living room. Friends and relatives visited the house all morning and into the early afternoon, but she tried to clear the late afternoon hours for her meeting with Jerry's buddies. Josh was stationed in the kitchen. If the doorbell rang, he was to answer it and tell the concerned visitors that his mother was resting. Mary wrestled with whether to have Josh join the conversation, but she was unsure what difficult-to-hear details would be revealed, so she asked him to hang out in the kitchen.

Mary placed two occasional chairs in front of the coffee table, which sat in front of the divan. The four of them were not uncomfortably close, but they were near enough to one another so they could talk softly and still be heard. To free his hands, Sammy placed Jerry's vest and net to the side of the divan as he sat down. "Jerry's camera is in the pocket," Sammy said, pointing to the vest. Mary sat to his right on the couch. Don and Chuck sat in the chairs with the coroner's bag between them.

"Before you begin, I have a question for you," Mary said. Is there anything in what you are going tell me that Josh shouldn't hear? He is in the kitchen. I'll ask him to join us if you think it's appropriate."

Don answered, "The only thing I can think of is Jerry's choice for the next keeper of the inkwell. He chose Josh. That may be something that you want to tell him, rather than us.

"So, there are no gruesome details that would upset him?

"No, what we have to tell you will add substance to your unique family tradition."

"Then I'll ask him to join us. You can tell him about his Dad's decision. He will be pleased, and hearing it from you will be meaningful, I think."

"Great," answered Chuck.

Mary went to the kitchen and returned with Josh. "Josh, you know these guys, I'm sure."

"Yes, I do."

The three men stood, greeted Josh with handshakes and hugs, and returned to their seats. Josh joined the circle in a dining room chair, which he placed next to his mother.

"They were with Dad when he died, and they want to tell us more about what happened," Mary explained.

"First thing first," Sammy said. He handed her the inkwell. "I removed it from Jerry's pocket just after we found him. It is all Jerry talked about for two solid days."

"Sammy's right," agreed Don. "And you know Jerry. He never talked much. I mean, he was always engaging and fun, but, you know, he never jabbered on. This trip was different. All he could talk about was Grandpa Reed and the inkwell and the stained pants and who he should name as the next keeper."

"He answered that question yesterday. He wanted you to be the next keeper, Josh," added Chuck.

"Josh, hang onto this, will you?" asked Mary as she handed Josh the inkwell. He smiled timidly, nodded, and clasped the familiar relic in his protective right fist.

"Congratulations, Josh. I don't need to tell you how important the job was to your dad. I'm sure you'll meet his expectations and then some. And I must tell you that something happened yesterday that was far beyond our own expectations," Chuck said as he picked up the bulging brown, paper bag.

"Jerry only told us the whole story twice, and we just wanted to make sure we understood something. Do you remember Grandpa Reed's stained pants?" Chuck asked. "How'd they get that stain?"

"He had the inkwell in his pocket. There was ink residue in the bottle, and as he swam to freedom, the residue became ink again. It leaked and stained his pant leg. Is that what Jerry told you?" Mary asked.

"Yes, exactly. Now, we can explain our strange behavior. When we found Jerry and pulled him to the shore, this is what we saw," Chuck explained. He opened the bag and carefully removed the contents. Jerry's wallet, his watch, his shirt, shoes, and pants. He unfolded the pants and laid them across the coffee table. The right leg, with its six-inch stain, was fully exposed.

"Oh, my God. Oh, my God!" Mary gasped. They all sat silently for a time. Sammy broke the silence.

"I removed the inkwell from Jerry's right-hand pocket after we brought him to shore. The empty bottle was in his pocket when he entered the water, and it was there when we found him."

"There is no explanation for the stain," Chuck said, trying to deter speculation.

"You know I disagree, Chuck. Mary, while your family has the inkwell, my family has the benefit of Scottish legends. For them, God was always nearby. Even a walk in the pasture might give you divine reassurance. They believed they lived under a giant, invisible dome. God controlled everything beneath the dome. They thought, if you accidentally walked close enough to the wall of the dome, you could rub up against a thin spot; a place in the wall that was worn so thin that it allowed you to be undeniably aware of the loving presence of God. But do you know what? Our ancestors weren't given the corner on thin spots. We can brush up against them too."

"That stain on Jerry's pants is not an ink spot. It's a thin spot. I believe God is telling us not to worry. He is saying, 'It's okay. Jerry is fine. I have him now, and I will take it from here. You just carry on.' Yes, indeed, this is a thin spot, just as sure as we're sitting here."

The room was silent again. Mary took Sammy's hand with her left and reached for Josh's with her right. Josh placed the inkwell on the coffee table alongside the stained khakis, took his mother's hand, and connected with Don, who joined with reluctant Chuck. Chuck avoided eye contact but completed the circle as he took Sammy's hand. They sat and wept. Sammy didn't intentionally bring them to tears. But that's what happened. They all cried. Even Chuck.

Of Signs and Miracles

CHAPTER SIX

The funeral plans, though emotionally taxing, were not complicated. The funeral home director asked the questions needing answers and then guided Mary to find what was right for her and her family. Dealing with the practical issues that surrounded Jerry's death was almost a relief, as she was weighed her options about how to tell his story. That was the tough part. She respected Jerry's dedication to family history. But she was always happily on the periphery. It wasn't her story; it was Jerry's. Under normal circumstances, Jerry's dedication to family history would have been nothing more than an interesting footnote at his funeral. The unexplained, ink-spot changed things. Now, it was a story with supernatural implications. Mary simply did not know what to do with it.

She knew she would eventually tell her family. What she could not come to grips with was whether the entire story should be revealed at his funeral. She decided to ask her pastor, Mike Blair, and her friend, Arlene. The pastor would give her a professional opinion. Arlene would give her advice based on their friendship and her small-town savvy.

The pastor came first. She was scheduled to meet with him anyway at 10:00 a.m. on Saturday to iron out some funeral-service details. He was a middle-aged, enthusiastic, but thoughtful, Presbyterian minister.

"Pastor Blair, before we get on with the funeral details, can I ask you a question? It's about miracles,"

"Miracles, is it? Please, what's on your mind?"

"This is a long story. You do have some time, I hope?"

"All day," he said, as he grinned and leaned back in his mesh-backed desk chair.

Mary started from the beginning. She told the Major Reed inkwell story without pause, with emphasis on Jerry's responsibility as the keeper of the family heirloom. She ended with Grandpa Reed's affection for his stained pants and the fact that he was buried in them. Then, she took a breath and asked, "Are you still with me? Exceptional story, isn't it?"

"Fascinating. I'm surprised I've never heard it before."

"Jerry was careful with that. He loved to talk about it, but he was careful not to bore people. Now, are you ready for the miracle part."

"Speak to me," he said.

She spoke slowly so she could remember and repeat all that she had heard. Explaining how Jerry's friends pulled him from the river was the hardest part to tell. She did it, but not without allowing herself to summon visions of Jerry lying wet and lifeless on the muddy bank of his favorite trout stream. She stopped twice to regain her composure and catch her breath. Then she removed the pants from their paper bag and lay them across the pastor's desk.

"These are the pants Jerry was wearing when he died. The empty inkwell was in the right-hand pocket when he went into the water and when they brought him out." She smoothed the stained portion of the right pant leg. "There it is; a stain on the right leg about six inches long, just like Major Reed's. Sammy, one of Jerry's fishing buddies, called in a thin spot. Do you know that Scottish legend?"

"The story that suggests you can be aware of God's loving presence if you brush up against a thin place in the imaginary wall?" asked Pastor Blair

"That's the one. Sammy suggested that the stain was a thin spot. He said it was God telling us that everything is okay. Jerry is with him now, and everything is all right. We should all just carry on." Mary paused, wiped her eyes, and looked directly into the pastor's eyes. "As simplistic as that sounds, I believe him. My question is simple. What should we do with the story? Should we share it at the funeral, or should it remain a family thing? You're the only person I've told."

"Wow!" the pastor said in a loud whisper. "Wow, Wow, Wow. Mary, I've run into what people consider miracles or signs a few times in my ministry, but never something quite like this. Certainly, they spent very little time talking about contemporary miracles when I was in seminary. What does your family think?"

"They don't know anything about it yet."

"Why not?"

"The time hasn't been right. Everyone will be home by tomorrow night. I'll probably tell them then. Besides, a large part of the story is Josh's selection as the next keeper of the inkwell. That must be a family announcement. I'll do both at the same time."

"Mary, miracles and signs are very personal things. Now, some will tell you that supernatural deeds of any kind are not being done in this age. There is no need, they say. Biblical miracles and signs are enough to prove the power and presence of God. We don't need new ones. I am not one

of those people. There are too many unexplainable circumstances in people's lives to deny that God is working with
us daily, and he wants us to know it. Still, your question
is valid. Should you share the wonder of this remarkable
experience, or should you use it only as private reassurance
and comfort for your family? If you tell the world, you will
undoubtedly be accused by some of going off the deep end.
Keep it private, and no one gets to share the joy of Jerry's
divine contact."

"You nailed it," Mary smiled. "There's something else.
What about the funeral itself? If we share the story at the
funeral, don't we run the risk of turning the whole thing
into a sensational disturbance, rather than a respectful remembrance of Jerry."

"There is that, though I think it could be done respect-
fully. There is also the question of time. It took you quite
a while to tell me everything you had to say. I'm glad you
did, but if you choose to tell the story, it will have to be the
centerpiece of the service. You'll have to drop some of the
traditional things, but that is perfectly okay if that's what
you choose to do."

"I don't know," Mary sighed.

"Why don't you do this. Put the question before your
family to see what they think. The details we were going to
pin down today can wait. See what they think. There is no
need for you to carry this load all by yourself. Call me by
Monday afternoon. That'll give us enough time to do what
we need to do, no matter what you decide."

"Thank you, Pastor. Just telling you the story helped
tremendously."

"You can't leave without a prayer. Should we?
"Absolutely."

The pastor sat silent for thirty seconds. Then he prayed.
He thanked God for His willingness to be present in their

lives and he asked for guidance for Mary, her family, and himself in decisions yet to be made about Jerry's funeral.

When Mary left the church, she was exhausted. She thought about canceling her afternoon meeting with Arlene but didn't. Arlene showed up at 2:30 p.m. Right on time.

"God bless you, Mary. How are you holding up?" Arlene said, as she came through the doorway and embraced Mary in a long hug. Then she took an arms-length step back, placed her hands on Mary's shoulders, looked her in the eyes, and said what only a true friend could say. "You look awful. You must be so tired."

"I'm beat. This all happened so fast. Plus, there is an issue that needs to be settled. That's why I called you. I want to see what you think about something. Please, let's sit."

As they walked into the kitchen and sat at the table, Arlene noticed that a pair of neatly folded Khaki pants laying to the side of the table. She did not ask about them.

"Do you believe in miracles or signs from God?" Mary asked.

"I guess I do. It's not something I've thought much about."

"Well, I'm right in the middle of one, and I need to know what to do with it," Mary explained. "Remember the missing inkwell? I found out where it went. Jerry took it with him fishing, and he had it in his pocket when he died. Which leads me to my miracle."

Mary didn't have to spend much time on the Major Reed story because Arlene had already heard it. She reminded Arlene of the importance of Grandpa Reed's stained pants, and explained the circumstances surrounding Jerry's death. Then she reached for the neatly folded khakis.

"When they pulled Jerry from the water, he was wearing these. He had the empty inkwell in his right-hand pocket." She unfolded the khaki fishing pants so that the six-inch stain was in full view. "This is what greeted Jerry's fishing buddies."

Arlene said nothing. She gently lifted the pants and then flattened them against the table so she could run her fingers over the stain. "What in the world?"

"Mysterious, isn't it?"

"I guess that's the right word. So, you are telling me that there is no explanation for this stain other than some shadowy connection to Jerry's dead relative?"

"Strange as it seems, that's right, which leaves us with a bunch of questions," Mary said. She paused, took a long, slow breath, and said, "I know this is a lot to take in, and I hesitate to ask you, but I will anyway. How do we deal with this at Jerry's funeral? Do you think we should talk about this mystery, this miracle, this sign publicly, or do we keep it as a family thing?"

"Geeze, I don't know," Arlene answered sternly, not because she was disgusted at being asked the question, but because she was genuinely baffled.

"Don't think about it too hard. Just give me a first-glance answer. What do you think?"

"I don't know. I guess I'd keep it in the family."

"Why?"

"It's very personal stuff. How are you going to make people understand Jerry's life-long attachment to the inkwell at a funeral? The whole Grandpa Reed story was fascinating when I first heard it, and, very honestly, it was sort of way out there. Add the fishing-trip ink stain, and it becomes off-the-charts weird. I believe it, Mary. But I have the advantage of knowing you and Jerry very well."

"Don't you think there's a dash of hope in the story that should be shared?" Mary asked.

"So many times, when I hear stuff like this, I think, 'Gosh, miracles never happen to me. What am I doing wrong?' That's selfish of me, I know. And I guess if it happens to you, and I believe it, it happens to me, too. Right?"

"I think so. If you believe it, it is as much yours as it is mine," Mary responded. "I've told this story twice. Once to you and once to the Pastor. As I have done that, I've become a little more comfortable with it. Thank you for listening. The kids will all be home tomorrow and, ultimately, what they think is right is what we'll do. But I must let the pastor know by Monday so he can plan accordingly. So, if you have any additional thoughts to share, please call me."

"Absolutely. Do you mind if I share it with Roger?"

"No, not at all."

Arlene left, and Mary removed her shoes to relax on the divan in front of the fireplace. She stared at the inkwell, which had found its way back to its designated high perch … until she fell asleep.

Horns of the Dilemma

CHAPTER SEVEN

Julia flew home from Chicago. She arrived late on Saturday night. Mary stayed up to greet her, but after shared hugs and quick tears, she excused herself.

"I'm just beat, Julia. I would love to talk more, but I would probably doze off. Do you mind if I turn in?"

"Not at all, Mom. We'll talk tomorrow. You go to bed."

"Okay. Your room is ready for you. Clean towels are on the nightstand. Goodnight."

Julia turned in too. She wept quietly for a long time after going to bed in her old room.

Robert arrived the next day at about 3:00 p.m. He chose to drive from North Carolina because he wanted time alone. Intermittent eruptions of grief added time to his journey. He had to stop to pull himself together several times, before driving on. Julia and Robert both thought they had no more tears to shed until they sat down with Mary and Josh later that afternoon. They ached their way through their first wave of collective sorrow. They said little, hugged a lot and wept.

Mary finally spoke. "There will be plenty of time for this. There is some business that we need to attend to."

"What business?" Julia asked, sounding more upset than she had meant to.

"I'm sorry. That was the wrong word. It's just that there are some funeral details I haven't pinned down. I need all your help to do so. I know it sounds trivial, but when you hear what I have to say, I think you'll understand," Mary explained.

"Okay, Mom. The floor is yours," Robert said.

"First, I must share the story of the circumstances surrounding your father's death. And I can't do that without reminding you of the story of our inkwell. Do you all remember Grandpa Reed's escape and the stain on his trousers?"

"Yeah, yeah. The inkwell leaked and stained his pants. Eventually, he came to love those stained britches and asked to be buried in them." Robert repeated from memory.

"Perfect. That's where we'll start. Your dad and I were preparing our will, but he stalled the process. We had a meeting planned with our attorney, and he canceled it because of his indecision about one thing." Mary took a breath. "He couldn't decide which one of you should become the next keeper of the inkwell. You'll remember he was the keeper for forty-five years, and it was very important to him."

"And what does that have to do with Dad's funeral?" Julia asked.

"I'm getting there. And this will take a minute, so bear with me. Your dad said he needed to focus, and what does he do when he needs to focus?"

"He goes fishing," answered Josh.

"You got it," Mary answered with a motherly smile. "But this time, he took the inkwell with him."

Mary spent the next few minutes explaining the fishing trip, the men he fished with, and the advice he sought from them. Then she described the heart attack, Jerry's drift down the river, and his retrieval.

"Now we are getting to the heart of the matter. When they brought him ashore, they saw this." Mary reached beneath her chair, brought forth Jerry's folded khakis. She unfolded them and lay them across the coffee table just as Sammy had done for her. She flattened the right pant leg against the table, providing a full, unwrinkled view of the stain.

"He had the empty inkwell in that pocket." Mary paused and let the reality of the stain sink in.

"What are you telling us, Mom?" Julia blurted. "This is nothing but eerie."

"Or heaven-sent," Mary smiled. "Dad's fishing buddy, Sammy, was certain of that."

Mary explained his thin-spot theory. She also discussed Pastor Blair's and Arlene's reactions. "So, here are the horns of the dilemma. Do we share this remarkable story about Dad's departure with the others at the funeral, or should it be reassurance and comfort for our family only? I want you to think about it. I know it will take some time to digest, but I must tell Pastor Blair what we want to do by noon tomorrow.

"There is one other thing. Now, I don't mean to throw this in as an afterthought. It certainly wasn't for your Dad. In fact, it was the reason for the fishing trip. On the last day of his life, he told his fishing buddies which of his children he had chosen to be the next keeper of the inkwell. It was a tough decision for him. He loved you all more than you can imagine. But, his fishing trip did what he wanted it to do. It allowed him to pass an important family responsibility to the right person. Josh will be the next inkwell keeper."

She got up, faced Josh, cupped her hands around his face, kissed his forehead, and headed for the kitchen. "I have to put the pizza in the oven."

The room was quiet for a very long time. Finally, Robert broke the silence.

"My God, that's a lot to think about. But there is no doubt that Dad chose the right person to be keeper. Congratulations, Josh. You're the perfect choice."

"I agree," Julia said. "Congratulations, Josh. You'll make us proud!"

"Thank you," Josh responded. "They told me about it yesterday. I haven't had time to think about it much. I'm too busy missing Dad."

"We are too, Josh. We are too," Robert agreed. "About the inkwell story, I think we should keep it to ourselves. Dad's death is a very personal thing. I think I'd like to keep the story that way too. Besides, how's anyone going to work that unbelievable story into a funeral service?"

"The whole thing is so personal," Julia added. "It is a story we've heard all our lives. The story has special meaning to us because we've lived with it for so long. But not many others have ever heard it. Will they get it like we do, or will they think we're all a bunch of superstitious loonies?"

"I wonder what Dad would want us to do?" Josh mused. "He loved the story, the tradition, and the uniqueness of it all. I don't know any other family who has such a story to tell."

"Remember, Josh, the story is different now," Robert said. "It isn't just a story of one family's fascinating history. It's a story about a supposed sign from God in the form of an ink stain on Dad's pants. That turns an ancestral tale into a mystical, spiritual statement. There's a big difference between the two."

"Do you believe it happened?" Josh asked.

"Probably. But nobody else will."

"So, you care most of all about what other people think?" Josh responded, using his recently practiced debate skills at a time that surprised even him. "But you do believe it, don't you?"

Robert paused, looked at Julia, and then back at Josh. "Yes, I guess I do."

"I do, too," Josh said. "I believe Grandpa Abram escaped from the British. I believe Grandpa Archie survived a duel. I believe that Silvia Miller heard an imaginary dog bark. And I believe that Dad's pants were mysteriously stained. And I believe, except for us, there was nothing more important to Dad than our family story. This new chapter would not change that. He'd want the story told."

"Yes, he would," agreed Julia. "And his funeral is his day, not ours. Who cares what people think?"

"You're probably right. Dad would want it told," Robert agreed. But it is easy for you and me, Julie, to be nonchalant about it. After the funeral, we'll be gone. Mom and Josh will be here, living with the fallout."

"Some bad, but some very good, I'll bet," said Josh.

No one spoke. Then Julia broke the silence. "Okay, let's tell Mom," Julia said.

Robert knew he was beaten. He agreed to tell the world about his father's miracle.

Caution to the Wind

CHAPTER EIGHT

"Pizza's hot," Mary announced. "Come and get it. Drinks are on the counter, and paper plates are the tableware of the day."

"Smells good, Mom," Robert said. "I think we have an answer for you."

"Good," Mary answered. "But let's wait until everyone is served, and we've said grace to revisit that question. It is just so good to look at you all together again." Mary filled her plate and sat in her usual seat, closest to the bay window. Everyone else followed suit by sitting in their unofficially assigned seats, the places they had occupied during their growing up years. That left one chair at the head of the table. It was Jerry's chair. They all stared at the empty seat and struggled to avoid tears.

"Hey, Josh, why don't you sit here. You're the keeper of the inkwell," Robert kidded as he motioned to Jerry's empty chair.

"No, thank you. If I sit there, I'll have to say grace."

Everyone laughed and held their tears at bay.

Mary said, "I'll say grace. But, wait a minute." She retrieved the stained khakis from the living room and hung them over the back of Jerrys' empty chair. Then she prayed, "Heavenly Father, thank you for your very evident presence in our lives. Please continue to stay close in the coming days. Please, stay very close. In Jesus' name. Amen."

Still chewing her first bite of pizza, Mary began the conversation. "Well, that didn't take long. I expected a lengthier deliberation. What are your thoughts? You said you think you have an answer?"

"Mom, you were right. There are reasons to share this story and reasons not to share it," Julia explained. "As we discussed them, it was apparent that most of the reasons not to share it stemmed from our concern about what other people would think. We decided that those concerns were not as crucial as another question. Josh, you're up."

Josh was surprised by Julia's unplanned handoff, but he responded as if their replies had been scripted. "Mom, the most important question is, 'What would Dad want?' He loved the inkwell story. He loved being the keeper. He loved that it was a big part of our lives. We think Dad's stained pants are as important to the story as any other part of it. Maybe even more important. In a way, they complete it, at least for him." Josh hesitated a moment as he stared across the table at the stained khakis. "Mom, we want to tell the world about what happened because we think it's what Dad would want us to do."

"Robert, you have been quiet. Do you agree?" Mary asked.

"Yes, I do," he answered. "We know how careful Dad was about telling the story. But that caution was not because he wanted to keep it a secret. He was cautious because he didn't want to bore people who weren't likely to appreciate the story. But if he thought they should hear it, he threw caution to the wind. We think that's what we should do now."

Josh and Julia made eye contact. They both raised their eyebrows in surprise and approval of their brother's newly found support for their point of view.

Mary nodded and looked around the table. "Good. That's what we will do. I'd come to the same conclusion, especially after the Pastor agreed that it could be done properly. I'm so glad you agree. I'll call Pastor Blair the first thing in the morning. Josh, will you get the Journal so I can give it to him. He'll need it to prepare his comments. I'm sure he'll do a good job. He is a good storyteller."

Josh had a different idea. "No, Mom. I want to do it," he said.

"You what?" she laughed. Then, realizing that her surprised response held an insulting measure of doubt, she doubled back. "Don't misunderstand, Josh. You know the story as well as anyone. And you speak as well as anyone. It just that this will be an emotional day, and there will be hundreds of people there. I don't want you to find yourself in an awkward situation. Remember how we wept so easily this afternoon. That same kind of thing can happen at any time. I'm about to lose it right now. Are you sure?

"I'm sure."

"He's right, Mom," Robert interrupted. "A family member must tell the story, and he's the one to do it. He can do it, and if he has a tough time, which I don't think he will, one of us will jump in to help. Let him do it. Remember, we are doing this for Dad. Dad made him the keeper, and he'll make Dad proud."

Mary hesitated, then acquiesced. She said, "Okay. By the way, Robert. Have you considered law school?"

Everyone laughed. Josh helped himself to another slice of pizza.

"Mom, do you remember the first time you saw the inkwell?" Julia asked.

"Yes, I do. I remember it well. I also remember Jerry's mother's advice about it. Jerry showed it to me about a month after we were engaged. We were at his house. He opened a little wooden box and removed a small velvet bag, which held the inkwell. He gave it to me and invited me to see what was inside. I did and was puzzled at first. Then he started to talk. When he finished, I loved him even more for the depth of his devotedness to his family history. That's something my family didn't care much about."

"Grandma Reed? She gave you advice about the inkwell?" Julia asked.

"Yes, she did. She took me aside one day and asked if Jerry had shown me the inkwell. I told her that he had and how impressed I was with his enthusiasm for its remarkable story. She looked me straight in the eye and said, 'Be prepared to make room for it. It is very important to Jerry.' She said, 'Don't be fooled by his quiet ways. When something adds interest and meaning to his life, he'll spin a permanent cocoon of affection around it.' Those were her exact words. I'll never forget them. She said that the inkwell was one such thing, and she was sure that I was too. I took her advice. It helped me, but I had no idea that making room for the inkwell would also be required at his funeral."

Filled with Wonder

CHAPTER NINE

The church was packed. Mary and the kids sat in the second row of the center section. The first row was unoccupied. Sammy, Don, and Chuck also sat near the front, in a pew to the right of the center section. Like Major Abram Reed, Jerry would be buried in his stained trousers. His closed casket was placed at the front of the church, just to the left of the pulpit. The room fell silent as Pastor Blair rose to speak.

"Good morning. We've gathered here today to remember Jerry Eugene Reed and to thank God for his wonderful life, which ended suddenly last week. Jerry sold men's clothing. But he did much more than that. He was an active member of the Rotary Club, he served as chairman of the Chamber of Commerce for a time, he coached baseball, he was an elder in this church. He sang in our choir. He was an avid fly fisherman. He and his wife, Mary, had three children. He was a very proud father. He was many things. Most of them we all knew about. Few of us knew about his duties as keeper of the inkwell. The inkwell is a family keepsake, handed down through generations of Reed descendants. The keeper of the inkwell is the person who looks after the inkwell during his or her lifetime. Jerry was his generation's keeper.

"Mary and I spoke at length about whether to tell Jerry's inkwell story this morning. Then she talked with her family. Because of a remarkable thing that occurred the day Jerry died, we all decided it was the best way to celebrate Jerry Reed. Jerry's son, Josh, will tell us more about it. But first, let's praise God with song." The choir rose and sang a heartfelt rendition of *Going Home*.

On cue, Josh walked to the pulpit. He was confident, poised, and comfortable. When he smiled, he looked a lot like Jerry. Many times, when you put teenaged boys in a suit and tie, they look awkward and uncomfortable. That was not the case with Josh. His self-assured manner put everyone at ease, especially his mother.

"Good morning. See this," he said, holding up the inkwell in the palm of his hand. A close-up image of the little glass bottle flashed on the projection screen behind him. "It is an inkwell that helped my fifth, great grandfather escape from the British during the Revolutionary War. It has been in our family for going on eight generations. The inkwell and the story behind it are important to our family. There were very important to Dad. He was the keeper for forty-five years."

Josh sat the inkwell on the front edge of the pulpit, the projected image behind him faded away, and he told the story of the inkwell. He was eloquent. His voice was strong. His eye contact with his audience was constant, as he spoke without notes. Everyone listened with interest and quiet admiration for his unusual maturity. He wrapped up the escape story giving full emphasis to Grandpa Reed's stained pants. Then he looked down at his father's coffin and prepared to talk about the miracle.

"Last week, Dad went fishing," he said, his voice wavering for the first time. "Last week, my father went fishing," he almost whispered. His voice cracked, his head was down, and his shoulders shook as he tried to choke back sobs from the sudden wave of grief.

On the outside chance that Josh would falter, Robert sat nearest the aisle so that he could reach the pulpit quickly. He wasn't quick enough. Chuck bounded up the short flight of stairs in two quick steps and stood with his arm around Josh before Robert could step into the aisle. Mary, who sat to Robert's left, saw him begin to stand and touched his arm with her right hand and motioned for him to sit with her left. Somehow, she knew that Chuck's surprising rush to help Josh was as it should be.

As always, if something needed doing, Chuck was the man to do it. He embraced Josh, moved him a step away from the microphone, and whispered in his ear. "Josh, you've done a great job, an outstanding job. Really, you have. And nobody cares that you've stopped for a second. How about this? Since I was fishing with your Dad when all this happened, why not let me tell this part of the story while you catch your breath. If I make a mistake, you can jump in and correct me. Okay with you?"

"Yes," Josh whispered. He was glad to leave the stage and to rejoin his family.

Chuck stepped to the pulpit, adjusted the microphone, and began, "My name is Chuck Randall. I was a good friend of Jerry's. In fact, I was fishing with him on his last day with us." He sensed that his audience needed some time to adjust to the speaker change, so he extended his introduction of himself.

"I've been trout fishing with Jerry for over twenty years. In all that time, Jerry never quit nudging me to find a church. In fact, he invited me to join him here many times.

I always found a reason not to come. Looks like he finally got his way, doesn't it?"

Quiet laughter rippled through the audience.

"As many of you know, I am a dentist. I have filled teeth for many of you. But Josh and I are not here to fill teeth. We're here to fill you with wonder. I think this remarkable story about Jerry's passing will do that," Chuck continued, as he looked down at Mary for her approval. She smiled and nodded. "You should know that Josh has promised me to jump in and correct me if I make a mistake.

"We went fly-fishing last Wednesday. We fished for two days, and Jerry couldn't quit talking about his grandfather's escape from the British and the inkwell. It was on his mind because he was trying to decide who should be the next keeper of the inkwell. As Josh pointed out, it was a job that Jerry held for forty-five years. It is no wonder that he was taking such care to pick the right person for the job. No one was surprised that he chose Josh. Jerry was the seventh person to care for the inkwell. Josh will be the eighth, and if his words this morning are any indication, he will do an excellent job.

"We didn't know it when Jerry invited us to go fishing, but the inkwell was the reason for the trip. Jerry was our levelheaded planner and our organizer. He would never call us on Tuesday and want to go fishing on Wednesday. Never in a million years. But, this time, he did. We soon found out why. He wanted to ponder his inkwell-keeper decision, and he wanted our company as he did it. He brought the inkwell with him to show it to us. There were three of us. He revealed the inkwell with absolute pride and enthusiasm."

Chuck explained Jerry's death as delicately as he could. He told about seeing Jerry's hat and the fly box floating downstream. He talked about finding him and bringing him ashore, though he skipped the part about dislodging his body from the submerged tree.

"When we brought him ashore, the inkwell was in his right-hand pants pocket," Chuck said and then paused. "Beneath it was a six-inch ink stain. A stain just like Grandpa Reed's. Let me repeat. It was an ink stain just like Grandpa Reed's. Except Jerry's stain came from an empty, ink-free, 250-year-old inkwell."

At that point, an image of the stained pants appeared on the projection screen. Chuck didn't know it was coming. It surprised him when the audience stirred, and he noticed people looking at the screen. He, too, turned and looked.

"There it is," he said, "Just as gloriously mysterious as the day we found him. Was that a miracle? Was that a sign? Let me tell you what Sammy thought it was. Sammy McCartney is a charter member of our fly-fishing quartette. He thought it was a thin spot."

Chuck explained the thin-spot theory almost as precisely and believably as Sammy had done. Then he asked Sammy and Don to stand so he could introduce them. He said that he thought that it was important to do so that the audience would know that he was not the only witness. At that point, the projected image of the stained pants disappeared.

"We all saw it, and our jaws all dropped. Was it a miracle or a thin spot or some other supernatural transgression against the laws of nature? I'll just call it a thin spot because my idea of a miracle is this: of all the fly fishermen in the country who I could have partnered with, I got to fish with Jerry Reed. I was one of three who was lucky enough to stand beside Jerry in a cold-water stream several times a year for more than twenty years. Most times, we caught trout. Sometimes we didn't. But we always had fun, thanks to Jerry. That is my miracle. He was a good man, a fair man, an honest man, a great dad, and one of the most pleasant people to be around that I have ever met.

"And he was a Christian. Anyone who knows me will agree that I have sort of a built-in contrary nature when it comes to spiritual matters. Well, I tried to pressure Jerry into defending his faith many times. He never took the bait. He would just smile and say, 'You'll figure it out, Chuck. You'll figure it out.' Jerry Reed was my miracle. I don't quite have it all figured out. But today, I can say thank God for the inkwell and thank God for Jerry Reed."

Chuck started to leave the pulpit, then stopped, stepped back to the microphone and said, "Josh, as the new keeper of the inkwell, how do you think we did?"

Josh's spontaneous response brought everyone to their feet. He smiled, stood up, and began to clap. He started a round of applause that the congregation of the First Presbyterian Church of Cedar Grove, Missouri, had never experienced at a funeral. It wasn't for Chuck. It was for Jerry, Mary, Julia, Robert, and Josh. Chuck stepped down, and Pastor Blair stepped to the pulpit to end the service.

"Miracles? Well, as Christians, we know all about them. We've got walking on water, a healed leper, we've got the loaves and the fishes, and many more. Is an unexplainable ink stain on Jerry Reed's khakis as important? In some ways, probably not. But in one significant way, it most certainly is. If it reminds us of the undeniable presence of a loving God, then it is every bit as important. The Bible tells us that the things that mark an apostle are signs, wonders, and miracles. Let us live as apostles. It isn't easy. Someone once said that miracles are numerous, but our perspectives are limited. Let us try to live as apostles. You see, to some degree, our perspectives are within our control. Albert Einstein put it this way. He said there are two ways to live your life. You can live it as though nothing is a miracle. Or, you can live it as though everything is a miracle. As for me, I'll take his second option. Let us pray."

His prayer was an emotional bookend for the unforgettable tribute to Jerry. As he finished, he asked the congregation to allow the family to exit first.

Trout Stream to Damascus

CHAPTER TEN

Chuck, Don, and Sammy didn't fish together again for almost eight months. They only went then because of Mary. She finally scrolled through the photos on Jerry's camera and found the picture of the four, smiling friends surrounding Don's Lunker Sundae. E-mail wouldn't do. She made prints, had them framed, and she and Josh delivered them to their homes. She sat in the car while Josh took them to the door. The lonesome fishermen decided it was time to take God's advice and carry on.

They left on a Tuesday for two days on their favorite trout stream and Margie's pork tenderloin sandwiches. Don drove, Chuck rode shotgun, and Sammy sat in the back seat.

"We've haven't seen much of one another since Jerry's funeral. How's everybody been?" Don asked.

"Nothing much new, though I did buy one of those rubber landing nets. They're supposed to be great because your hook can't get caught in the net. It would be nice if Jerry were here to see it. He was hard to keep up with when it came to new stuff. It would be fun to go one-up on him." Chuck said.

"That he was," agreed Sammy. "It'll be odd fishing the Blue Hole without him. Gosh, the more I see of Josh, the more I notice how much he's like Jerry. Did you get to talk to him much when he brought the picture over?"

"No, not much. He was just kind of in and out. Mary was in the car and gave me a big wave. It was nice of them to do that, wasn't it? The picture's hung directly above my fly-tying desk." Don said.

"Real nice," agreed Chuck. "I did get to talk to him a bit. Mary even stepped in for a moment. They both seemed fine, cheerful, and pretty much back to normal. But, gosh, I was impressed with Josh. Didn't he do a wonderful job that day? Just to try, it took courage. And then to stand up there and tell that story without a note before him. He was something."

"You didn't do a bad job either, my friend. In fact, I thought you were exceptional. What in the world motivated you to get up there and stand-in for Josh?" Don asked. "I think it surprised the hell out of Mary and her kids. Did you see the look on Josh's brother's face?"

"No, I didn't. My back was to him. Was he surprised?"

"Shocked is a better word. He started to stand when he saw you bolt for the stage. His jaw dropped, and he turned and looked at Mary. She raised her palm and lowered it slowly, as if to say, 'Wait, let's see what happens.' He sat back down."

"Very honestly, I was probably as stunned as he was. After Josh left the stage and I stood behind the pulpit, there was a terrifying moment when I wondered what I had just done and what I was going to do next. I looked down at Mary. She gave me what I thought was a smile of approval, and I started talking."

"Well, I agree," said Sammy. "You turned what could have been an awkward service into a blessing for everyone who attended. Plus, you kept Josh engaged and in the limelight. It was as if the whole darned thing was planned. Yet, I know it wasn't. How'd you do it?"

"Wait a second, Sammy. Did you just call me a blessing?"

"Don't let it go to your head. Just answer my question."

"How did I do it? I've wondered about that myself. To be honest, I responded to Josh. My heart broke for him as he choked up. All I can tell you is that I saw him hurt, and I hurt. I had to do something. I never considered that it wasn't my place to help him. All I knew was he was having trouble telling the story. Who the hell wouldn't? As mature as he seemed when he began, he was a sixteen-year-old boy who had just lost his father. I jumped up there out of concern for him. Where did the words come from? I'm unsure. Somehow the words just came. They just came. That, in and of itself, is a bit of a miracle."

"When you think about it, it turned out as it was supposed to turn out. Josh's big brother probably knew the story but not well enough to nail it like you did." Sammy added. "It took courage for Mary to allow the inkwell story to be the focal point of Jerry's funeral. But what you did was essential. Are you sure you didn't feel Jerry prodding you on? Maybe he wanted you to get up there and do it."

"Sammy, I love you, but you are a perennial thin spot. Yes, you are. You are a thin spot."

"Well, I'd say that Jerry Reed's funeral was a resounding success," Don said.

"Do you know what else was successful?" Chuck asked. "Jerry's quest for a Journal entry as interesting as any of the others. He did that in spades. Now, he paid a high price to do it, but he did it."

"I guess Mary or Josh will write the Journal entry. I wonder if they've done that yet?" Don said.

"I'll bet they have," replied Sammy. "And if they tell it like Chuck did, it'll be perfect."

"I know, I am such a blessing," Chuck said.

Sammy ignored Chuck's sarcasm and said, "Yes, you are. Yes, you are."

The three fishing buddies made their obligatory stop at Margie's before hitting the stream. It was breakfast time, so she wasn't there. But their Lunker Sundae picture was. It was off to one side of Margie's Lunker Board. There they all were, surrounding Don's ice-cream mountain. The photo had a hand-drawn circle around Jerry's head and torso. The typed note thumbtacked beside it read, "In remembrance of Jerry Reed, who died on stream, September 7th, 2018. An excellent fisherman and a wonderful man. We will miss him."

"What a perfect sentiment," commented Chuck. "Jerry's quiet strength and kindness touched everybody, didn't it?"

They would fish the Blue Hole first. They put on their waders and strung their rods atop the hill. They were ready to fish. Chuck bounded down the single-file path first. Sammy was next in line, and he purposely walked slowly. He wanted to speak with Don privately, and his slower pace separated them from Chuck just enough to do so.

"Chuck seems different, don't you think?" Sammy whispered.

"Yes. I couldn't help wondering what had gotten into him during his talk at Jerry's funeral. And he does seem a little more at peace than usual."

"Think I should ask him about it?"

"What will you ask him?"

"Well, I guess I'll ask him if he believes in God."

"You do that at your own risk," Don warned.

"Still, if the time is right, I think I'll do it," Sammy responded.

Don took the fast water beneath the short waterfall. Chuck took the middle water, which pooled into a slower, deeper flow, and Sammy took the end of the pool near the riffles. Almost simultaneously, they all caught fish. Sammy and Chuck netted their fish and waited for Don to complete his prolonged retrieval. Once his fish was in the net, they gathered on the bank to compare the size of their fish before they released them. Chuck had the largest fish.

"Thank you, Jerry," Chuck said, saluting the sky with his fly rod.

Sammy couldn't help himself. He took three steps out of the water, leaned his rod against a branch, and sat on a low rise. It was almost the same spot where Jerry, Chuck, and Sammy had stood to heckle Don during his drawn-out lunker catch. He sat because he anticipated an extended conversation about Chuck's apparent changed opinion.

"Chuck, there is one other thing that I've meant to ask you," Sammy said.

"What's that?" Chuck answered as he swished his net in the stream's clear water to clean the trout slime from it.

"Based on what you said during Jerry's funeral, and during our conversation today, it appears that you have changed your mind about God's existence. Is there some truth to that?"

"Maybe so. Maybe so," Chuck said. "Hey, let's move to the Cliff Hole. Let's see if Jerry's up there too." He left the stream and started a quick-time walk up the path to the Cliff Hole and its foliage-covered boulders.

Sammy and Don followed without saying another word. Sammy knew he should have waited to ask his question over a pork tenderloin at Margie's, where there was no place for Chuck to flee. He also knew that faith journeys often occur in fits and starts. There was no question; Chuck had changed. Even though his new perspective didn't produce the trout-stream-to-Damascus response that Sammy had hope for, it was clear that Chuck's journey had begun. Jerry was right. Chuck would figure it out.

A Meeting with Sylvia

CHAPTER ELEVEN

Mary asked Josh if she could write Jerry's Journal entry. He agreed. "Mom." He said. "It's yours to write. I'd love to read it when you finish, but it is yours to write. Honestly, I'm glad you're willing to do it. I'll write the next one. Okay?"

"Okay," Mary agreed with a smile.

It was easier than she had anticipated, though she didn't do it without a thoughtful assessment of the job at hand. She didn't backslide. She was sure the family's decision to speak publicly about Jerry's ink-stained khakis was the right thing to do. She felt that way even before she received dozens of phone calls and cards from people who thanked her for telling Jerry's story. Pastor Blair called too. He said the service was one of the most heartwarming and inspirational he had ever witnessed. And everyone thought that Josh was something special. But it was one thing to offer mystical reflections at a one-time, transitory event like a funeral. It was quite another to commit them to the permanence of a written document. The last thing she wanted to do was to submit Jerry to the same mocking winks and eye rolls that people gave superstitious, old Silvia Miller and her imaginary barking dog and inkwell clairvoyance.

Then Mary thought about the bold consensus that her children had come to around her kitchen table on the Sunday evening before the funeral. She thought, too, about the clear-eyed, youthful courage that guided Josh to the pulpit. Then she thought of Jerry and laughed at herself. She was certain that Jerry had made friends with Silvia the day before yesterday. The thin-spot incident became part of the official record.

It was Josh's turn to be the keeper of the inkwell.

TIM BROWN

The Inkwell reflects Tim's appreciation of history, his passion for fly fishing, and his appreciation of good friends. He weaves playful dialog, plot-twisting surprises, and a challenge to faith into this mysterious story. He learned to write succinctly as an advertising copywriter and his fiction benefits from that discipline, although it's wrapped in the easy-to-read flair of a master storyteller.

He holds a BA in journalism at the University of Nebraska and an MA in mass communications from Denver University. Between degrees, he served as a journalist in the U.S. Army.

Book Club
Questions

1. Is there something like the inkwell in your family?

2. Jerry goes fishing when he needs to think, what do you do when making a decision like this? Is it similar or different to Jerry's?

3. Would your guidelines for choosing the next keeper be similar or different to Mehitable Reeds? How so?

4. What advice would you give to Jerry in deciding on the next keeper? How does it compare to the advice his buddies gave?

5. Jerry says of Chuck several times, "He'll figure it out." What do you think he means by this?

6. Would you have waited for Jerry's pants to be released to tell Mary the story? Or would you have told her earlier?

7. How did the discussion of miracles in this book impact you?

8. What choice would you have made regarding sharing the story of the inkwell at Jerry's funeral?

9. How do you think these experiences will impact Chuck's spiritual journey?

10. If you had to write a journal entry for Jerry, what parts of his life and story would you include?